¿Qué hay en el cielo, querido dragón?

What's in the Sky, Dear Dragon?

por/by Margaret Hillert
ilustrado por/Illustrated by David Schimmell

NORWOOD HOUSE 🏠 PRESS

Queridos padres y maestros:

La serie para lectores principiantes es una colección de lecturas cuidadosamente escritas, muchas de las cuales ustedes recordarán de su propia infancia. Cada libro comprende palabras de uso frecuente en español e inglés y, a través de la repetición, le ofrece al niño la oportunidad de practicarlas. Los detalles adicionales de las ilustraciones refuerzan la historia y le brindan la oportunidad de ayudar a su niño a desarrollar el lenguaje oral y la comprensión.

Primero, léale el cuento al niño; después deje que él lea las palabras con las que está familiarizado y pronto, podrá leer solito todo el cuento. En cada paso, elogie el esfuerzo del niño para que se sienta más confiado como lector independiente. Hable sobre las ilustraciones y anime al niño a relacionar el cuento con su propia vida.

Sobre todo, la parte más importante de la experiencia de la lectura es ¡divertirse y disfrutarla!

Shannon Cannon

Shannon Cannon
Consultora de lectoescritura

Dear Caregiver,

The *Beginning-to-Read* series is a carefully written collection of readers, many of which you may remember from your own childhood. This book, *Dear Dragon's Day with Father*, was written over 30 years after the first *Dear Dragon* books were published. The *New Dear Dragon* series features the same elements of the earlier books, such as text comprised of common sight words. These sight words provide your child with ample practice reading the words that appear most frequently in written text. The many additional details in the pictures enhance the story and offer the opportunity for you to help your child expand oral language skills and develop comprehension.

Begin by reading the story to your child, followed by letting him or her read familiar words and soon your child will be able to read the story independently. At each step of the way, be sure to praise your reader's efforts to build his or her confidence as an independent reader. Discuss the pictures and encourage your child to make connections between the story and his or her own life.

Above all, the most important part of the reading experience is to have fun and enjoy it!

Shannon Cannon

Shannon Cannon,
Literacy Consultant

Norwood House Press • P.O. Box 316598 • Chicago, Illinois 60631
For more information about Norwood House Press please visit our website at
www.norwoodhousepress.com or call 866-565-2900.
Text copyright ©2014 by Margaret Hillert. Illustrations and cover design copyright ©2014 by Norwood House Press, Inc. All rights reserved. No part of this book may be reproduced or utilized in any form or by any means without written permission from the publisher.
Designer: The Design Lab

LIBRARY OF CONGRESS CATALOGING-IN-PUBLICATION DATA

    Hillert, Margaret.
      ¿Qué hay en el cielo, querido dragón? = What's in the sky, dear dragon? / por Margaret Hillert ; ilustrado por David Schimmell ; traducido por Queta Fernandez.
        pages cm. -- (A beginning-to-read book)
      Summary: "A boy and his pet dragon look at both the day and night skies. They learn about the sun, moon, animals, and airplanes that move through the sky. This title includes reading activities"-- Provided by publisher.
      ISBN 978-1-59953-610-1 (library edition : alk. paper) -- ISBN 978-1-60357-618-5 (ebook)
      [1. Sky--Fiction. 2. Dragons--Fiction. 3. Spanish language materials--Bilingual.] I. Schimmell, David, illustrator. II. Fernandez, Queta, translator. III. Hillert, Margaret. ¿Qué hay en el cielo, querido dragón? IV. Hillert, Margaret. What's in the sky, dear dragon? Spanish. V. Title. VI. Title: What's in the sky, dear dragon?
      PZ73.H5572072 2014
      [E]--dc23

                        2013034966

Manufactured in the United States of America in Brainerd, Minnesota.
240N—012014

¿Qué hay en el cielo, querido dragón?
¿Qué hay en el cielo?
Por la noche podemos ver algunas cosas.

What's in the sky, Dear Dragon?
What's in the sky?
We can see some things at night.

3

Mira allá arriba. Mira allá arriba, papá.

Look up. Look up, Father.

Mira allá arriba, a lo lejos.

Look way, way up.

Veo algo amarillo.
Es lindo. Es grande.
Nos da luz.

I see something yellow.
It is pretty. It is big.
It gives us light.

Sí, sí.
Esa es la luna.

Yes, yes.
That is the moon.

También veo unas lunas pequeñitas.

I see some baby moons, too.

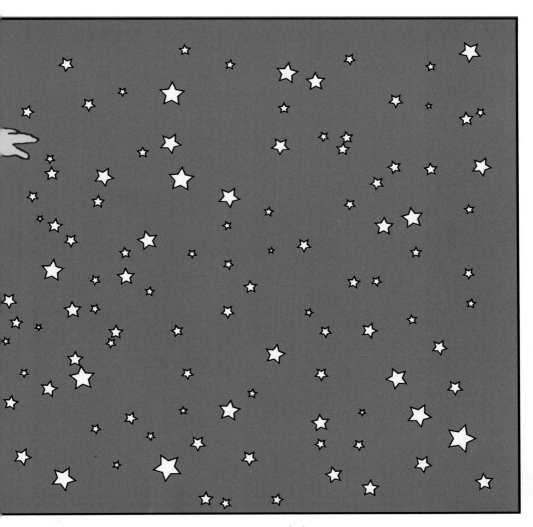

No, no.
No son lunas.
Son estrellas.
También nos dan luz.

No, no.
They are not moons.
They are stars.
They give us light, too.

9

¿Son estrellas las chiquititas?

Are the little, little ones stars?

No. Son luciérnagas.
Puedes tomar algunas para mirarlas,
pero luego debes soltarlas.

No. They are fireflies.
You can get some to look at,
but then put them back.

Oh, mira allí.
Al búho le gusta el cielo de noche.

Oh, look here.
The owl likes the night sky.

Y mira eso.   And look at this.
¡Oh, mira eso!   Oh, look at this!

¡Qué divertido!   What fun!
¡Qué divertido!   What fun!

15

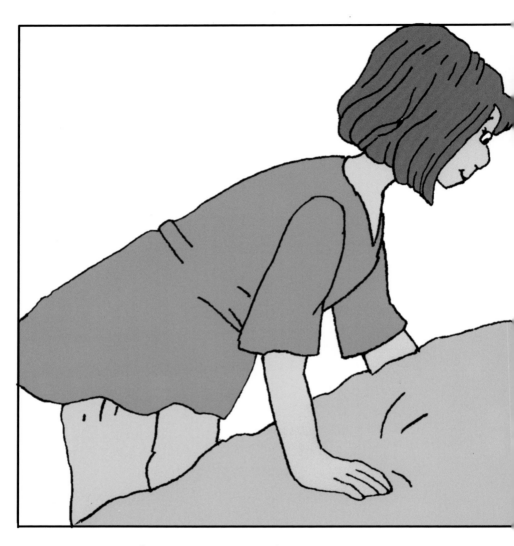

Ahora vamos a la cama.

We will go to bed now.

Cuando nos despertemos,
miraremos el cielo de día.

When we wake up,
we will look at the day sky.

Ahora lo que vemos es el sol.

Now what we see is the sun.

El sol es grande, grande, grande.
Nos da luz y ayuda a que las cosas crezcan.

The sun is big, big, big.
It gives us light, and helps things grow.

Las nubes están en el cielo.

Clouds are in the sky.

La lluvia también está en el cielo.
La lluvia está en las nubes oscuras.

Rain is in the sky, too.
Rain is in the dark clouds.

Algunas veces, la lluvia y el sol crean un arcoíris, un arcoíris muy, muy lindo.

Sometimes the rain and sun make a rainbow. A pretty, pretty rainbow.

Veo rojo y anaranjado.
Veo amarillo, verde y azul.

I see red and orange.
I see yellow and green and blue.

23

Los pájaros también están en el cielo.
También son lindos.
Mira como vuelan.

Birds are in the sky, too.
They are pretty too.
Look at them go.

Un avión está en el cielo.
Es como un pájaro grande.
Puede ir lejos, lejos, lejos.
Podemos irnos lejos con él.

An airplane is in the sky.
It is like a big bird.
It can go away, away, away.
We can go away with it.

Estamos en el avión.
Nos iremos, iremos, iremos.

We are in the airplane.
We will go, go, go.

Tú estás conmigo
y yo estoy contigo.
Es divertido estar en el cielo, querido dragón.

You are here with me.
And I am here with you.
It is fun to be in the sky, Dear Dragon.

READING REINFORCEMENT

The following activities support the findings of the National Reading Panel that determined the most effective components for reading instruction are: Phonemic Awareness, Phonics, Vocabulary, Fluency, and Text Comprehension.

Phonemic Awareness: The /s/ sound

Substitution: Ask your child to say the following words without the **/s/** sound:

sat - /s/ = at	spot - /s/ = pot	Sam - /s/ = am
sand - /s/ = and	she - /s/ = he	said - /s/ = aid
share - /s/ = hare	sin - /s/ = in	stop - /s/ = top

Phonics: The letter Ss

1. Demonstrate how to form the letters **S** and **s** for your child.

2. Have your child practice writing **S** and **s** at least three times each.

3. Ask your child to point to the words in the book that start with the letter **s**.

4. Write down the following words and ask your child to circle the letter **s** in each word:

see	sad	this	sky	say	was
set	clouds	shapes	miss	something	sip
ask	guess	star	said	house	sun

Vocabulary: Story Words

1. Write the following words on separate pieces of paper:

   sun   birds   stars   rainbow   airplane

2. Say the following sentences aloud and ask your child to point to the word that is described:

   - This gives us light in the day sky. (sun)

   - These animals have wings and can fly in the sky. (birds)

   - These twinkle and give off light in the night sky. (stars)

   - What colorful thing could you see in the sky after it rains? (rainbow)

   - What did the boy and Dear Dragon get on to go away in the sky? (airplane)

Fluency: Echo Reading

1. Reread the story to your child at least two more times while your child tracks the print by running a finger under the words as they are read. Ask your child to read the words he or she knows with you.

2. Reread the story, stopping after each sentence or page to allow your child to read (echo) what you have read. Repeat echo reading and let your child take the lead.

Text Comprehension: Discussion Time

1. Ask your child to retell the sequence of events in the story.

2. To check comprehension, ask your child the following questions:

   - What can you see in the sky at night?

   - What does the sun give to us?

   - Have you ever seen a rainbow? If so, where?

   - What other things can you see in the sky?

ACERCA DE LA AUTORA

Margaret Hillert ha escrito más de 80 libros para niños que están aprendiendo a leer. Sus libros han sido traducidos a muchos idiomas y han sido leídos por más de un millón de niños de todo el mundo. De niña, Margaret empezó escribiendo poesía y más adelante siguió escribiendo para niños y adultos. Durante 34 años, fue maestra de primer grado. Ya se retiró, y ahora vive en Michigan donde le gusta escribir, dar paseos matinales y cuidar a sus tres gatos.

Photograph by Glenna Washburn

ABOUT THE AUTHOR

Margaret Hillert has written over 80 books for children who are just learning to read. Her books have been translated into many different languages and over a million children throughout the world have read her books. She first started writing poetry as a child and has continued to write for children and adults throughout her life. A first grade teacher for 34 years, Margaret is now retired from teaching and lives in Michigan where she likes to write, take walks in the morning, and care for her three cats.

ACERCA DEL ILUSTRADOR

David Schimmell fue bombero durante 23 años, al cabo de los cuales guardó las botas y el casco y se dedicó a trabajar como ilustrador. David ha creado las ilustraciones para la nueva serie de Querido dragón, así como para muchos otros libros. David nació y se crió en Evansville, Indiana, donde aún vive con su esposa, dos hijos, un nieto y dos nietas.

ABOUT THE ILLUSTRATOR

David Schimmell served as a professional firefighter for 23 years before hanging up his boots and helmet to devote himself to work as an illustrator. David has happily created the illustrations for the New Dear Dragon books as well as many other books throughout his career. Born and raised in Evansville, Indiana, he lives there today with his wife, two sons, a grandson and two granddaughters.